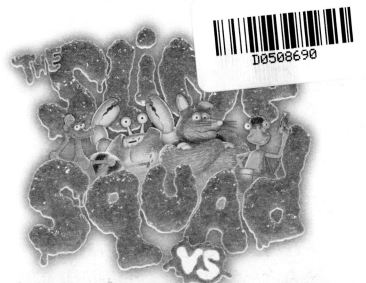

THE ALLIGATOR ARMY

by Steve Cole

Illustrated by Woody Fox

RED FOX

THE SLIME SQUAD vs THE ALLIGATOR ARMY
A RED FOX BOOK 978 1849 41397 8

Published in Great Britain by Red Fox Books,
an imprint of Random House Children's Books
A Random House Group Company

This edition published 2011

1 3 5 7 9 10 8 6 4 2

Red Fox Books are published by Random House Children's Books,
61–63 Uxbridge Road, London W5 5SA

www.**kids**at**randomhouse**.co.uk

Addresses for companies within The Random House Group Limited can
be found at: www.randomhouse.co.uk/offices.htm

THE RANDOM HOUSE GROUP Limited Reg. No. 954009

A CIP catalogue record for this book is available from
the British Library.

Printed in the UK by CPI Bookmarque, Croydon

For Isabella Kench

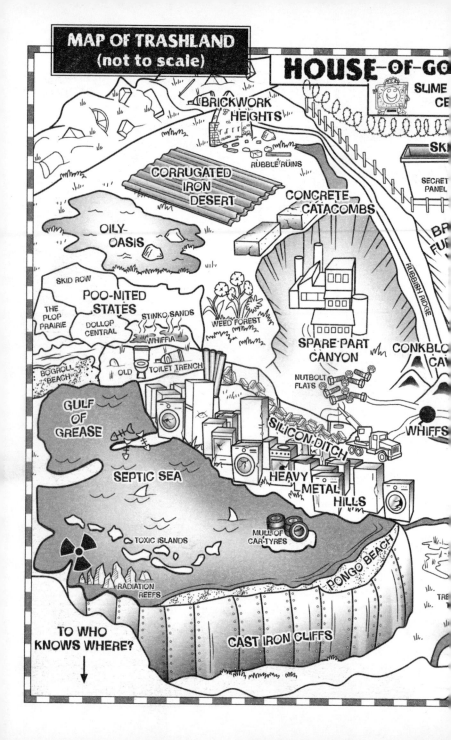

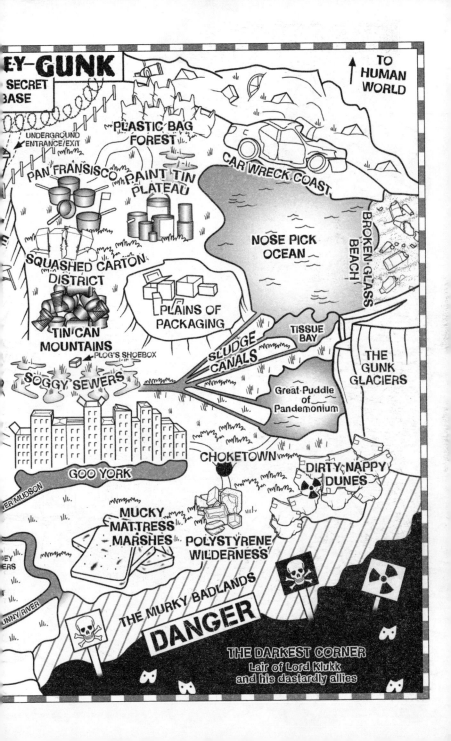

ONCE UPON A SLIME...

The old rubbish dump was far from anywhere. An enormous, mucky, rusty landscape of thousands of thrown-away things.

It had been closed for years. Abandoned. Forgotten.

And then Godfrey Gunk came along.

Godfrey wasn't just a mad scientist. He was a SUPER-BONKERS scientist! And he was very worried about the amount of pollution and rubbish in the world. His dream was to create marvellous mutant mini-monsters out of chemical goo – monsters who would clean up the planet by eating, drinking and generally devouring all types of trash.

So Godfrey bought the old rubbish dump as the perfect testing-ground and got to work.

Of course, he wanted to make good, friendly, peaceful monsters, so he was careful to keep the nastiest, most toxic chemicals separate from the rest. He worked for years and years . . .

And got nowhere.

In the end, penniless and miserable, Godfrey wrecked his lab, scattered his experiments all over the dump, and moved away, never to return.

But what Godfrey didn't know was that long ago, tons of radioactive sludge had been accidentally dumped there. And soon, its potent powers kick-started the monster chemistry the mad scientist had tried so hard to create!

Life began to form. Amazing mini-monsters sprang up with incredible speed.

Bold, inventive monsters, who made a wonderful, whiffy world for themselves from the rubbish around them – a world they named Trashland.

For many years, they lived and grew in peace. But then the radiation reached a lead-lined box in the darkest corner of the rubbish dump – the place where Godfrey had chucked the most toxic, dangerous gunk of all.

Slowly, very slowly, monsters began to grow here too.

Different monsters.

Evil monsters that now threaten the whole of Trashland.

Only one force for good stands against them. A small band of slightly sticky superheroes . . .

The Slime Squad!

Chapter One

BEWARE THE LAIR

The mist was thick as cold grey custard, and the wind howled like a hundred scalded cats. Struggling through the gloom came Plog the monster, his orange fur on end, his long ears flapping in the gale. How long had he been trudging through these Murky Badlands? It felt like for ever ...

Plog glimpsed something dark and massive up ahead.

The fog parted for a few seconds to reveal a ramshackle castle made of old packing crates painted night-black and blood-red. Fenced in by barbed wire, it looked fearfully forbidding.

"At last!" Plog turned and yelled: "Guys, come quickly. Lord Klukk's secret stronghold – we've found it!"

Plog's team-mates – Furp, Zill and Danjo – came running out of the misty wilderness. Together they were the Slime Squad, squelchy superheroes who protected innocent monsters all over Trashland.

And right now, they looked extremely apprehensive.

Not long ago they had finally beaten

their worst enemy – the evil criminal chicken mastermind Lord Klukk – for good. His plans to conquer Trashland had come to nothing, but his secret lair still remained, lost in the sinister fringes of this wild and whiffy rubbish-dump world . . .

Until now.

Furp, the sticky frog-monster with the big brain and even bigger metal pants, surveyed the fortress ahead of them.

"Getting inside won't be easy," he murmured. "Klukk will have left traps behind for the unwary."

"But we *have* to break in," said Zill, a sassy six-legged poodle-skunk with a big bushy tail. "Klukk may have gone, but his base must be stuffed full of gruesome gadgets and evil experiments." She shook her head and set her poodly pompoms rocking. "We can't risk some other wannabe evil genius pinching it all to keep up the bad work. Just imagine what they could do!"

"I'd rather not." Danjo, a crimson crab-monster, raised his big pincers. "Enough hanging about – let's sort this place out!" He strode off through the fog on his three sturdy legs, heading for the high fence. "Luckily I've got built-in wire cutters . . ." He closed his pincers on the taut barbed wire. *TWANG!* The fence parted, and a high whistling note sounded – like something falling . . .

"Look out!" yelled Plog. He dived at Danjo, knocking him clear as – *THUNK!* – a massive spear dropped

down from above and spiked deep into
the mud where the crab-creature had
been standing.

"Whoa!" Danjo gulped. "Thanks,
Plog – I was almost crab-on-a-stick!"

Furp hopped over. "I suggest we go
carefully from now on."

"*Very* carefully," Zill agreed. "I'll try
to open the door from here." She judged
the distance to the castle's thick steel
door. Then, like a fisherman casting a
line, she spat a sticky strand
of slime towards it.
SPLAT! The end of her
slimy rope struck the
metal – and burst into
electric crackles! Zill
quickly dropped the
slime-line, and it fell
smoking to the
ground . . .

Setting off a hidden
landmine just ahead of them!

KROOOM! The deafening explosion sent the Squaddies staggering. Danjo swiftly raised his right pincer and squirted out a thick shield of icy slime to protect them from the worst of the blast.

"Good work, Danjo," Plog murmured. "That was too close."

"A diabolical trap," Furp agreed. "Klukk fixed it so that anyone who made it through the minefield would get zapped by the door instead."

"So how *do* we get inside?" asked Danjo, lowering his icy shield.

Plog threw a clod of mud at the door. This time nothing happened. "Hmm, looks like the door's run out of zap-power. Zill, try hitting it with another slime-line to make sure."

"You're the boss, Fur-boy." Zill coughed up another slimy

strand and, with a jerk of her head, slung it at the door. This time it stuck — and Plog tied the other end to the upright spear.

"There!" he declared. "Now we can dodge the mines by walking this tightrope all the way to the entrance!"

Furp went first, hopping carefully across. Zill scampered on all six of her tippy-toes. Plog and Danjo clung to the slimy strand like pegs to a washing line, shinning their way across to the door. They were big as monsters went, and their backs scraped perilously close

to the minefield below. But finally they made it over and stood beside their friends.

Plog studied the front door. "Is this the only way in?"

Effortlessly, Furp scaled the side of the castle with his sticky hands and feet. He peered around, then hurried back down. "There are no other doors or windows that I can see."

"Then we'll just have to risk any booby traps that might be behind this thing." Plog looked down at his heavy iron boots – then kicked the door with all his strength. *KLANNGGGG!* The metal slab was smashed off its hinges and slammed to the floor . . .

To reveal a growling, scaly beast in

the hallway ahead of them! It looked to be part alligator and part wolf, with tough green skin, glaring red eyes, and jaws that bristled with fangs.

It stood in front of a large wooden door, barring the way.

"Uh-oh," said Danjo. "I think we've just found Klukk's guard dog!"

"It must've been cooped up for ages!" Zill spat out a slime-line and lassoed it around the creature's neck. "Come on, Fido – here's your lead, it's time for walkies!"

But the beast didn't like its sticky collar. It shook itself wildly – with such force that Zill was sent crashing into the wall!

"Bad move, gator-wolf!" said Plog, helping the dazed Zill to her feet. "Danjo – give our unfriendly hound the hot slime special!"

"Coming right up!" Danjo sloshed the sinister sentry with a steaming blast. But the gator-wolf simply caught it in its mouth, gargled – then advanced threateningly.

"I've got an idea," said Plog. "Furp, can you distract it?"

"Let's find out!" With blistering speed, Furp began bouncing between the walls, zooming over the snarling creature's head.

The gator-hound swiped at him and clawed the walls where Furp had landed as if trying to wipe off the frog-monster's footprints.

Meanwhile Plog pulled off his heavy metal boot. It was full of water – it had to be, because whenever Plog's ugly great tootsies were exposed to the air . . .

"Quick, Zill," groaned Danjo. "Cover your nose – before Plog's slime flows!"

The gator-wolf roared and advanced on Plog – then went cross-eyed. Revolting yellow slime was already dripping from Plog's unpleasant toes, and the stench was strong enough to floor an elephant. Plog flicked his foot, and a big gloopy drop splatted over the animal's head. With a shriek and a roar, it fled past Plog and rushed outside, Zill's slime-line still trailing from its neck. It cleared the mines, landed by the barbed-wire fence and vanished into the fog, making strange barking noises.

"Well done, Fur-boy!" cheered Zill, as Plog put his yucky foot back into his boot. "You scared it away!"

"I suppose I must have," said Plog thoughtfully. "But that noise it made as it left – it almost sounded like laughter . . ."

Still sticking to the ceiling, Furp pressed on towards the wooden door at the far end of the hall. "Come on, let's see what it was guarding."

Carefully he pushed open the door. Plog clenched his fists, Zill reared up on her two back legs and Danjo held out his pincers – all of them ready for anything . . .

But instead, they found –

"Nothing!" Furp frowned. "This room is empty!"

Zill checked all about. "You're right. No mean machines or weird inventions. The whole place has been cleared out."

Danjo and Plog stared in puzzlement. Sure enough, the vast metal chamber

had been
stripped bare.

"But why
would that
gator-hound
stay here to
guard an
empty room?"
Danjo
wondered.

"I have no
idea." As Plog
walked into
the room, the
door swung closed behind
him – to reveal an envelope taped there.

"Hey, look!" Zill pulled it off. "It's
addressed to us."

"Careful, Zill!" Furp plucked it out of
her paws. "It might be another trap."

"I'll open it," said Plog bravely. He
pulled out the piece of paper inside
and read:

Dear Slime Squad,
Thank you for giving me all I need – you fools!
Yours disagreeably,
D.O.S.

Danjo scratched his red head. "What's that supposed to mean?"

"Who or what is D.O.S.?" Furp added.

"And how did they know we'd be coming?" said Zill.

"I have no idea," said Plog, feeling oddly unnerved. Even now, he thought he could hear the scaly wolf-thing's sinister sniggering in the distance. "But I have a feeling that sooner or later we're going to find out!"

Chapter Two

MAKE IT SNAPPY

Plog sat quietly as
Zill drove the
Squaddies home in
the Slime-mobile,
their super-
charged invisible
transport. He
couldn't stop
puzzling over
D.O.S. and his
mysterious note.

"I'm sure the All-Seeing PIE
will have the answers," said Danjo when
they reached their secret cellar
headquarters.

Zill parked, and Plog led the charge to ask PIE his opinion.

"Ah, there you are," boomed PIE tetchily. "About time!" His name was short for Perfect Intelligent Electronics; not only was he an amazing super-computer, he was the Squad's big boss. He had sensors scattered all over Trashland, which meant that he could detect trouble anywhere at any time – and send the Squad off to sort it out.

"PIE," said Plog, "we found Klukk's old base in the Badlands – but weird stuff happened . . ."

PIE listened in silence as Plog explained.

"It seems to me," said Furp, "that this D.O.S. – whoever or whatever it may be – was the one who removed everything from Lord Klukk's base."

"But how did they get past the traps without setting them off?" wondered Zill. "How did they dodge that dodgy 'guard dog'?"

"Yeah," said Danjo, waving the mocking note. "And what does D.O.S. even mean?"

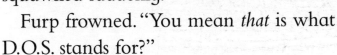

"Drain our sink!" PIE squawked suddenly.

Furp frowned. "You mean *that* is what D.O.S. stands for?"

"No," said PIE, "I mean the sink's

blocked up with potato peelings and the water is starting to pong. So drain it!"

Danjo sighed, scooted over and blasted the offending scraps with sizzling slime.

"But you must have some idea of what's going on, PIE?" said Plog.

"Of course," PIE replied. "To answer your question, Zill, it is obvious how D.O.S. got past those traps and obstacles. They were simply not there when he – or she, or it – emptied the place. D.O.S. then set the traps for whoever followed, and left that animal locked inside."

"But D.O.S. must've expected us to get past those obstacles, 'cos he left us the note," Plog pointed out. "So why bother?"

PIE remained silent, question marks drifting across his cracked screen.

Then, suddenly, his built-in alarm went off, and they were replaced by exclamation marks. "Warning! Robbery in progress at Quarkly's rank bank in Pan Francisco. Green reptile monsters detected . . ."

Zill gasped. "Like that 'guard dog'?"

"We'd better get on the case," said Plog, running back towards the Slime-mobile. "'Cos when danger looms large, the Slime Squad shout CHARGE!"

And charge they did, all the way to the cookware metropolis of Pan Fransisco. Here, old pots and pans and utensils had been turned into shops and houses – and Plog saw that Quarkly's rank bank was based inside an upturned deep-fat fryer. Little greasy monsters were fleeing in panic, but he could see none of the green reptiles PIE had reported.

As Zill brought the Slime-mobile to a screeching halt outside the rank bank, Plog piled out with

Danjo and Furp. "Let fear disappear," he cried, "the Slime Squad is here!"

"Thank gonkness!" A small orange monster bustled up to him. "The crooks are inside. They've gone downstairs to our underground vault – where all the money is kept."

Zill jumped down from the invisible vehicle to join her team-mates. "We'd better get checking."

"And then we'll get *decking*!" Danjo thumped his pincers together to stress the point. "Bad guys, beware. Let's go!"

Plog led the way inside the rank bank and paused beside a set of steps.

exit

Trashland's

cash was printed on used toilet paper – the whiffier the wad, the more it was worth – and Plog's sensitive snout told him that there was a fortune down here. "We'd better be ready for anything," he whispered.

21

Zill, Furp and Danjo nodded gravely, and padded down the steps after him.

The downstairs room was hollowed out of thick clay. Dozens of safes of different shapes and sizes studded three of the walls, and a gigantic bank vault dominated the fourth. The thick steel door hung open, and Plog could see a dozen green monsters moving about inside, each as big as he was.

They looked like crocodiles or alligators, but walked upright on scaly legs. Oddly, the reptiles wore black shorts, with a ragged black tie around their necks.

More oddly still, they didn't seem to be stealing the money at all. They were simply picking it up and chucking it out of the vault.

Plog took a deep breath and leaped down the last few steps. "Hold it, you lot – the Slime Squad's here!"

The twelve reptiles paused. Then they filed out of the vault to face the Squaddies, yellow eyes agleam.

"Let's not be rash – put down all that cash," growled Danjo.

"We've caught you robbers red-handed," Zill added.

"Well, *green*-handed, really," Furp continued, swallowing hard. "But you know what we mean."

"No we don't!" came a slithery yet commanding voice from inside the vault. "My gators aren't ssssstealing this money. We are merely *moving* it."

Plog blinked as an extraordinary figure stepped out in front of them. He was an alligator too, walking upright like the others, but he wore a wide-brimmed black hat, an eye-mask and a dark, swirling cape. He carried a diamond-topped cane in one claw, but his brilliant white teeth shone brighter than any precious stone.

"I am the Duke of SSSnap," hissed the oddly-clothed creature, his eyes shining. "Do I understand you have a problem with us being here?"

"I've got problems with your dress sense," Plog retorted. "You look ludicrous!"

"Sssays the bear-rat with sssomeone else's shorts on his head!" The Duke of Snap smiled. "Yes, Plog, I know all your sssecrets – *and* those of your sssilly SSSquad mates."

"Wait a minute," Furp muttered. "Duke of Snap . . . D-O-S!"

Zill felt a shiver down her tail. "You think he's the one who left the note?"

"There's no doubt," said Plog grimly. "Check out his pet!"

Danjo's jaw dropped – and those of the other Squaddies weren't far behind it – as the same scary gator-wolf which had fought them last night came scuttling out of the bank vault with a black box in its teeth. "Groarrrrr," it snarled, and dropped the box at the Duke's feet.

"Thank you, SSSabre," said Snap. "Good boy."

"All right, Snap," said Plog. "We know you've been inside Lord Klukk's secret lair. Why did you leave us that weird thank-you note?"

"Wouldn't you like to know!" Snap sniggered, and so did Sabre.

"What were you doing in Klukk's old place?" Zill demanded.

"I live in the Badlands too." Snap swished his cape. "Klukk was one of my neighbours. And when I heard he'd left Trashland, I helped myself to all the sssinister sssubstances and dastardly devices he'd left behind." He picked up the black box and smiled. "Now all his sssecrets are *my* sssecrets."

"How about you share the secret of what you're up to in that vault?" said Plog. "Whatever it is, it can't be good."

"You're quite right." Snap flicked open the cover of the black box to reveal a big red button, and giggled with glee.

"I'm going to blow it up!"

The Duke hit the button. Sabre and the gators all dived to the floor . . .

BWAMM! The explosion rocked the rank bank to its foundations and a ferocious fireball burst from inside the vault. Plog knew he was staring death in the face. But suddenly the floor – weakened by the blast – split open beneath him.

"*WAAAAH!*" Plog and the other Squaddies fell through the crack and plunged into nothingness . . .

Chapter Three
END OF THE SLIME!

Desperately, Zill coughed out a slimy safety net to stop her friends falling. It just managed to hold their weight as the flames scorched overhead.

"Well spat, Zill," said Furp, and Plog and Danjo nodded gratefully.

"This gator crime caper doesn't make sense," said Zill. "Why would Snap and his gang break into a rank-bank vault just to blow it to bits?"

"We have to find out." Plog waited till the flames had died down, then climbed stealthily up the side of the crevice. "I don't know who this Duke of Snap thinks he is, but— *Oomph!*"

As Plog stuck his head out of hiding, a gator appeared and squirted yellow goo into his face! Eyes stinging, Plog fell back down into the net, knocking his friends over.

Danjo looked up angrily – and another gator squirted purple goo into *his* face!

"Hey!" Zill tried to scramble up the muddy wall as Plog had done – and walked straight into a faceful of grey slime fired from yet another gator. As Furp hopped up to help her, a green spurt of goo caught him in the kisser – "Urgh!"

Danjo wiped his eyes. "What *is* this stuff?"

"I don't know." Plog shook the gunk from his face. "But now they've made me *really* mad!"

Using Zill's slimy net like a trampoline, he sprang up out of the crack and landed on two of the gators, squashing their stomachs with the soles of his iron boots. Then he whacked the other two with the backs of his furry paws, sending them flying across the ruined room.

Plog saw that the whole place was sooty and smoking, and that big bundles of banknotes had been burned to ashes.

Three more gators came scuttling
towards him – but then Danjo bounced
out of the crack in the floor and
squirted icy slime in their path. They
slipped over and landed on their
scaly bottoms.

"Quickly!" Plog
reached down into
the crevice to
help Zill get
out, while Furp
hopped up beside him.
"We can't let some goop in our
eyes stop us from getting these goons!"

"It won't." Zill was fuming with rage.
"That stuff they sprayed on me has
stained my lovely leotard. I'll have those
gators' guts for garters!"

"Hold off the Slime Squad, my
gators!" rasped the Duke of Snap, who'd
ducked back inside the vault. "I have
found what we came here for – now we
must take it away . . ."

Snap's gator brigade took up defensive positions around the smoky room. Then they pulled pistols from their shorts and opened fire. *BANG! PEE-YOWWW!*

"Ooof!" A sharp spike bounced off Furp's crash helmet. "They're firing *teeth* at us!"

"Those things sting!" cried Danjo, caught up in a hail of tooth-bullets. He quickly whisked up more slimy ice to use as a shield, and his fellow Squaddies sheltered behind it as fangs pinged off in all directions.

"Zill," said Plog, "I think it's time these gators felt some whiplash."

"Understood!" Zill stuck her head up over the shield and spat out a long slime-line. Then she cracked it like a sticky whip against the gators' knuckles.

The reptiles hissed and howled as the pistols dropped from their stinging paws.

"Now! Attack!" Plog broke cover to rush the remaining reptiles, his furry fists swinging. "Squad — Snap's our real target. We've got to get to the vault!"

Furp hopped through the air into the ranks of the enemy, braining gators with his big metal pants. Danjo fired hot slime into scaly faces, and Zill kicked out in a fury of furry paws. Sabre the gator–wolf growled and hissed — but Plog pulled off one boot and was soon sloshing the beast with more of his stinky foot-slime. The monster ran back whimpering to its master in the vault.

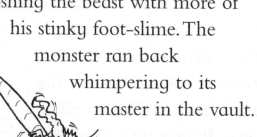

"Don't worry, SSSabre –
our work is done." The
Duke of Snap sounded
jubilant. "The heli-gator is
coming!"

Plog turned anxiously
to his team-mates. "Heli-
gator?"

The next moment, the
rusting roof above the
vault exploded and a fierce
wind whipped through the
rank bank. Shielding his
eyes, Plog stared up in
amazement. A huge green
helicopter was hovering
overhead – shaped like an
enormous alligator!

"Lower the winch," Snap snarled. "Fight on, my gators – we only need a little more time!"

"Well, you're not going to get it," cried Plog. As his friends kept fighting the remaining reptiles, he strode towards the Duke. The caped creep was standing in a deep crater, on top of something buried in the soil – something off-white that gleamed like ivory. "I don't know what you've found down there, but it stinks – I can smell it over the whiff of my foot-slime!"

"Can you?" Snap just laughed, his cloak billowing in the gale whipped up by the heli-gator's rotor blades. "Or perhaps your foot-ssslime has *ssstopped* sssmelling. Perhaps your foot-ssslime has SSSTOPPED ALTOGETHER!"

Plog looked down at his foot – and saw that it was clean and dry. "My slime!" he gasped. "Where's it gone?"

"Don't worry, Plog," Danjo shouted, running over. "I've got slime to spare.

Enough to share!" He aimed his hot pincer at Snap – but only a tiny dribble came out. "Huh?" He tried again with his cold pincer – but again, nothing happened. "I don't get it!"

"And ssso I *won't* get it!" chuckled Snap. A giant grappling hook attached to a thick rope had swung down from the heli-gator, and now the masked villain fixed it to the big white thing in the ground. "What a pity – for you!"

Suddenly Plog saw that Sabre was ready to spring. "Look out, Danjo!"

Danjo automatically raised his pincers to fire – but again, nothing came out. The ferocious beast leaped towards the two Squaddies and knocked them right out of the shattered vault. Plog shoved his remaining boot into the monster's mouth, trying to jam its jaws.

But even as he struggled, he heard Zill cry out in alarm. Turning, he saw her standing in a corner, surrounded by armed gators. She was trying to spit out a slime-line and swing away – but couldn't cough up a single strand. "What's wrong with me?" she wailed. "I've lost my slimy powers!"

"So have we!" shouted Danjo, grabbing Plog's other discarded boot and pushing *that* into Sabre's mouth as well.

"I'm in trouble too!" Furp yelled. He'd been climbing a wall to escape a group of gators, but now he was slipping back down again. His foes were firing teeth up at him, the molar missiles bouncing off his big round pants. "Owwww! Help!"

"We can hardly help *ourselves*!" Danjo groaned – but then Snap whistled and Sabre broke off his attack, trotting back to his master with both Plog's boots for trophies.

Covered in slobber and panting for breath, Plog glared at the Duke. "What have you done to us, Snap?"

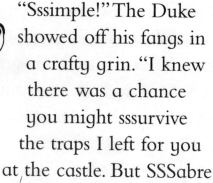

"Sssimple!" The Duke showed off his fangs in a crafty grin. "I knew there was a chance you might sssurvive the traps I left for you at the castle. But SSSabre was the deadliest trap of all. Each of you attacked him last night – kindly giving him a sssample of your ssslime as you did so. He returned to me with those sssamples and I ssstudied them closely . . ." He chuckled. "Then, using equipment ssstolen from Klukk's lab, I devised a ssspecial anti-ssslime ssserum –

which my hench-gators have sssquirted
in your faces!"

"So that's what hit us," Plog muttered.

"And now you are powerless to prevent
my rise to glory!" Snap struck a dashing
pose beside the grappling hook, one claw
on his hip, the other wielding his cane.
"Come, my gators! The SSSlime SSSquad
is defeated – and another part of the
grand design is ours!"

"The grand design?" Furp
twittered. "Bless my bonkberries!"
The heli-gator was rising
into the air – lifting as it did
so a colossal animal bone!
The Duke was
perched on top of
it, swishing his
cape. Sabre stood
by his side, with
Plog's mangled
iron boots still
in his mouth.

All the other gators jumped
aboard the dangling bone,
jeering at the Squaddies.

Zill spat and
spat, but couldn't
flick out even a
drop of slime.
"They're getting
away!"

Plog nodded helplessly as
the heli-gator and its
sinister cargo departed.
"And without our powers,
we can't do a thing to
stop them!"

Chapter Four
POWERLESS!

The four Squaddies trooped miserably up the steps to the ground floor of the ruined rank bank.

"I've never felt so helpless," groaned Danjo. "It looks like this is the end of the Slime Squad."

"The *Squad*, you mean." Zill sniffed. "We haven't got any slime now, remember?"

"We can't just give up," Plog argued, looking down at his bare feet. "The people of Trashland need us to protect them!"

"No, they don't," said Zill. "They need superheroes – which we aren't! Not any longer!"

The rank-bank manager was waiting with a crowd of onlookers and monsters from the press. As Plog led the Squaddies outside, cameras flashed and newspooper reporters surged forward.

"We saw the alligator-men's amazing helicopter," burbled a one-eyed blue monster. "Why didn't you stop them?"

Plog shrugged miserably. "We tried, but . . ."

"Did they take lots of money?" asked another.

"Dear me, no!" cried Furp. "It, er, all burned to ashes."

The rank-bank manager fainted. More camera flashes went off.

"We'll beat the gators next time,"
Plog told the crowds. But the sadness
and disappointment on so many
monstery faces was too much for him to
bear, and he quickly led his team into
the Slime-mobile.

Furp hopped straight
into the lav-lab –
a toilet-cum-
laboratory in the
back of the vehicle,
chock full of useful
gizmos and multi-
grade goo. "No wonder
Snap thanked us." He sighed.
"We gave him the secrets of our slime
on a plate!"

"Or on an alligator-wolf thing,
anyway," Plog agreed.

"He completely tricked us," groaned
Danjo.

Furp nodded absent-mindedly,
gathering beakers and Bunsen burners.

"Well, we should change out of our costumes."

"You're right!" Zill wriggled out of her dirty golden leotard and threw it on the floor. "We don't deserve to wear them now."

"That's not what I meant," said Furp. "When Snap squirted his anti-slime over us, he stained our costumes, right? So if I can take samples of the stuff and reverse its chemistry ..."

"You could make *anti*-anti-slime!" A hopeful smile spread slowly over Plog's face. "Do you really think you can do it?"

"I hope so." Furp scraped green goo off his crash helmet. "Though it may take a while."

Plog nodded moodily. "We'd better hope that whatever Snap is up to, he takes his time about it . . ."

But over the days that followed, the Duke of Snap proved that he was in no mood to hang about. The heli-gator was sighted all over Trashland. And while Furp worked on a cure for the anti-slime, all Plog, Zill and Danjo could do was sit and wait. PIE kept them up to date with the latest news reports on Snap's activities.

On day one the reptiles started an avalanche in the Tin Can Mountains to unearth another bone.

On day two Snap spread panic through the Paint Tin Plateau, overturning half-empty tubs to get at a small bone in the multi-coloured mud beneath.

And on day three he spoiled hundreds of holidays at the Gulf of Grease when Sabre and the gator-men drank the water dry – to reveal yet another mysterious bone, half buried in the gooey, sandy bed.

"This is driving me crazy!" Plog cried, slumped on a cardboard sofa. "I hate just sitting around while those grotty gators do what they like."

"Me too." Danjo picked up a slightly rusty rifle. "Even our slime-shooters are useless – because we don't have any slime to put in them!"

"I know." Zill wiped a tear from her eye with her tail.

"We never imagined we'd ever stop being slimy, did we?"

"I used to dream of having sludge-free tootsies," Plog admitted. "But you guys showed me what I could do with my goo . . ."

"Hey, I do the rhymes" – Danjo sighed – "while Snap does the *crimes*." He got up, crossed to the Slime-mobile and banged on the door. "Oi! Furp! Any closer to finding a cure?"

"Getting there," called Furp.

"That's what you said yesterday," Zill called back.

"Whoops!" There was a loud *BANG!* from inside the Slime-mobile, and Furp started coughing. "Er, I'm *sort of* getting there, anyway. Bit of a detour . . ."

Danjo buried his face in his pincers. "Terrific."

"You may have lost your slimy powers," PIE boomed behind them, "but you still have your minds. I suggest you use them."

"You're right," said Plog. "We need to ask ourselves *why* the Duke of Snap took away our powers."

"Easy," said Zill. "So we can't stop his 'rise to glory'. He told us that himself."

"Yes, but what did he mean by it?" Plog scratched his head. "Why is he tearing Trashland apart just to dig up these old bones . . . ?"

Danjo shrugged. "Maybe he has a big dog who's really hungry?"

"We've already met his pet," Zill reminded him. "What are those giant bones anyway? Any idea, PIE?"

"I've got a lovely idea," PIE answered. "We should go on a picnic with some worms."

"Er . . . yes," said Plog, "but have you got any idea about Snap's old bones?"

"Oh." PIE's screen blushed red. "They appear to be animal bones. But as for which animal . . . I am checking my memory banks for matches."

Zill looked at him suspiciously. "You mean you don't know."

"PLASTIC BAGS!" yelled PIE, so loudly that the roof rattled and the Squaddies jumped in the air.

"What is it, PIE?" asked Plog, his heart thumping.

"Do you need us to do some shopping?" Danjo wondered.

"I've just seen it. A bone . . . Barely visible beneath the grimy white layers of the Plastic Bag Forest . . ." PIE's screen was cluttered with exclamation marks. "But yes, definitely a bone!"

Plog gasped. "If it's buried there, then sooner or later Snap will come and pinch it."

"And probably trash the whole area," added Danjo.

"But," said Zill, "if we can take the bone before *he* does, it might spoil this grand design of his."

Plog nodded excitedly.

52

"And that'll buy Furp more time to find the cure for Snap's anti-slime."

"Best of all," said Danjo, "we won't need our slime to get hold of it – just a bit of brute force to dig it up, and the Slime-mobile to haul it back to our base!"

"There! Not so useless after all, are you?" said PIE.

"But we'd better get shifting," said Plog grimly. "The Duke of Snap could be coming for that bone at any moment!"

Chapter Five

BAGS OF DANGER

The Squaddies ran over to the Slime-mobile and bundled inside. The air was thick with smelly smoke and bright yellow bubbles.

Zill wiped the fogged-up windscreen with her tail. "I'll have to drive with the windows open!"

Plog peered through the smoke. "Where's Furp?"

"Here!" The frog-monster was wearing a gas mask and mixing murky liquids in the lav-lab's toilet. "What's going on?"

"PIE's found a bone," said Danjo. "We're going to dig it up before the Duke of Snap gets his claws on it."

"But I'm at a vital stage of my research!" Furp complained. "I've discovered that Snap's anti-slime came in four different colours because each was a different formula – specially made to affect each one of us."

Plog groaned. "So it's not just one cure you need to find – it's four!"

"How long will that take?" asked Danjo, as Zill started the engine.

"Perhaps five hours," said Furp. "Or perhaps five months!"

"Well, I'm going to get to this bone in the Plastic Bag Forest in five *seconds*," Zill growled. "Hang on!"

She floored the accelerator and the Slime-mobile sped off, faster than a bolt of lightning.

"Whoa!" Without his heavy boots to anchor him, Plog tumbled backwards onto the floor. Danjo clung onto his seat while Furp jammed his bottles and

beakers inside his pants and wedged himself in the toilet bowl.

Then, suddenly, Zill slammed on the Slime-mobile's brakes. This time Plog found himself catapulted to the front of the vehicle, and conked his head on the windscreen. "Ow!"

"Don't complain, Fur-boy." Zill helped him up. "We've arrived!"

Rubbing the bruise on his head, Plog opened the door and gazed out. The forest was a strange, desolate place. Strips of grubby plastic hung like flags from a thousand sticks and grass-stalks. They billowed eerily as the breeze brushed against them.

Danjo pushed his way out behind Plog. "Where's this bone, then?"

"Shouldn't be far away." Zill jumped down with a computer print-out from PIE.

"Apparently it's near a big yellow shopping bag. Let's get looking."

"Good luck," called Furp, staying put in the lav-lab, while Zill led Plog and Danjo on the bone hunt.

"It should be somewhere around here," she murmured. "Past those broken coat hangers ..."

"I see yellow!" bellowed Danjo, pointing a pincer ahead.

Sure enough, Plog could see a big bright bag waving in the wind. He ran towards it ...

And fell over something, landing right on his snout. "Ouch!"

"That's it!" Zill's tail shot straight up in the air. "The big bone – you just tripped over it!"

"Talk about stumbling on a great discovery," said Plog, getting back up. He could see now – there was something large, white and smooth sticking out of the dirt. "That looks like one end of the bone. Big, isn't it?"

"Big or not, that bone's coming home!" Danjo flexed his largest pincers and used them to shovel through the thick mud.

Zill joined him, digging furiously with four paws. "I hate to think what the Duke of Snap is doing with all these bones."

"They're full of calcium and stuff for healthy teeth," said Plog, grunting with effort as he helped clear the soil. "Perhaps Snap and his gators are eating the things themselves!"

The Squaddies worked solidly for an hour or more, digging and burrowing while the carriers kept up their ghostly rustle.

"This thing's longer than I expected," Zill admitted. "Wider too."

Plog nodded and shook sweat from his fur. "Let's see if we've loosened it at all."

Zill and Danjo lent him a paw and a pincer. Together, they heaved and tugged and pulled and yanked and wiggled and woggled and strained and struggled – but they couldn't budge the colossal bone.

"It's no good," Plog panted. "We'll never shift it like this. What we need is heavy machinery. Something like—"

"A helicopter with a big winch and grappling hook," gabbled Zill.

"Yeah, that'd do it," Danjo agreed.

"It wasn't a suggestion." Zill was staring up into the sky. "It was an observation. Look!"

Over the rustling of the carrier bags, Plog suddenly realized he could hear the drone of motors and rotors. A dark green shape had swung into sight high above them. "The Duke of Snap's heli-gator!" he groaned.

Danjo banged a pincer crossly on the bone. "We weren't quick enough!"

"The bone's still stuck fast," Plog reminded them. "Snap's gators will have a job to take it."

But suddenly two sleek, dark missiles blasted out of the heligator and came streaking towards them.

"Uh-oh!" Danjo whipped out a pincer and tried to create an icy slime shield – but of course, no slime came out. "Sorry. Old habits die hard."

"But we'll die easy if those things hit us!" cried Zill. "What's Snap doing? He'll blow up his bone!"

"He must be trying to dig it loose the quick way," said Plog, pushing his friends into the trench they'd dug around the giant bone. "Come on, take cover!"

The missiles whooshed into the ground beside them. *KER-WHOOOM!* The explosions hurled mud up to the sky. Flimsy scraps of plastic filled the air like confetti. Plog didn't think the ground would ever stop rumbling.

"That was too close," said Danjo. "A few more shots like that and he'll have blown his bone loose all right – and us to pieces!"

The heli-gator dropped down lower, its rotors whipping up the plastic bags into a frenzy of fluttering.

"I'll try to draw Snap's fire away from you by running over to the Slime-mobile," said Plog. "You head into the Plastic Bag Forest and find some cover. I'll grab the slime-shooters, then come and join you."

"But we've got no slime to put in those things," Danjo reminded him.

"Furp must have something in the lav-lab," said Plog. "Now, good luck – and keep your heads down."

"Will do," Zill whispered, and Danjo nodded. "You be careful, Fur-boy."

With a brave smile, Plog jumped out of the smoky trench and sprinted for the invisible Slime-mobile. He pushed through blades of grass and leaped over rubbish in his way. The heli-gator's engines changed pitch as it suddenly sped up to follow him – and the sinister *whoosh* of another missile soon followed.

Plog looked over his shoulder to see
Zill and Danjo running off into the
flimsy forest – and the deadly projectile
zooming towards him at frightening
speed . . .

Chapter Six
A TASTE OF TROUBLE

Plog quickened his pace, pushing himself
to the limit. He scrambled up onto a
grassy hillock as – *KA-KRAMMM!* –
the missile exploded behind him,
blasting him high into the
air. Plog tumbled
helplessly towards
where he knew
the invisible
Slime-mobile
was parked . . .
  But just
before he
could crash
into the side,

Furp opened the door – and Plog crashed into *him* instead. Both monsters tumbled inside.

"Plog!" Furp groaned. "I was just coming to find you."

"Lucky for me you did," Plog panted. "Snap can't see the Slime-mobile – outside or in. With any luck he'll think that last explosion got me."

"Snap's here?" said Furp anxiously. "I heard the blasts, but I didn't know what was happening. Where are Zill and Danjo?"

"I think they're safe for now," said Plog. "Snap is trying to dig out the bone by firing missiles close beside it. I came here to grab the slime-shooters – it's the only way we can fight back."

"Perhaps not." Furp scrambled up.

"Plog, I was coming to tell you – I think I've almost completed your cure!"

Plog's ears shot up in the air. "You have?"

"Here!" Furp grabbed a smoking, foaming beaker that smelled like a woodlouse farting on a dead hedgehog. "Gulp it down."

Plog eyed the beaker nervously. "You said it wasn't finished."

"Oh yes." As another explosion went off outside, Furp put a pinch of yellow powder into the beaker. The smell grew worse – as if a raccoon had done a wee on the woodlouse before it farted on the dead hedgehog. "There we go!"

Deciding he'd better swallow the drink before Furp could make it smell any worse, Plog held his nose and glugged it down.

For a moment nothing happened.

Then Plog's brain seemed to flip like
an electric pancake and his throat felt
like burning bats were flapping up and
down it. His eyes bulged, his head spun,
his teeth rattled and his
fur did a Mexican wave
from his toes to his
dribbling nose.

"Whoa!" he
gasped, pointing at
the beaker. "That . . .
that stuff . . ."

"Good, was it?"
Furp smiled knowingly.
"Well, that should be
enough to cure you. Unless I'm
totally wrong, in which case it'll just
give you the runs."

Plog stared at him. "*What?*"

Furp almost overbalanced as another
loud explosion rocked the Slime-mobile.
"I'll have the runs myself if this keeps up.

Do your feet feel any different, Plog?"
he asked hopefully. "Can you feel them
sliming up?"

"No," Plog admitted. "I can't."

"Oh . . . I could've sworn that formula
would restore your slime!" Furp sighed.
"Perhaps I should just throw away the
cures I'm making for the rest of us . . ."

"Don't give up. You'll find the answer,
Furp." Plog gulped as the noisiest
explosion yet shook the vehicle. "Now, I
must get back to Danjo and Zill with
fully-loaded slime-shooters."

"Fill them with the lav-lab's toilet
water," Furp suggested. "It's not been
flushed for two days."

"Better than nothing."
Plog grabbed the
shooters and filled
them with the whiffy
water. More and
more explosions were
going off outside.

"Sounds like Snap is blasting the whole Plastic Bag Forest to ashes. But now we can at least try to fight back."

"Shall I come with you?" asked Furp.

"No, keep working on the cures," Plog told him. "We *must* get our powers back!" With one slime-shooter in his hands and two more tucked under his arms, he took a deep breath – and then pushed open the door and ran back into the noise and smoke outside.

The heli-gator was swooping in circles like a batty bird of prey, firing missile after missile. The carrier bags were half buried in sticky mud thrown up by the blasts. Through a curtain of dust, Plog saw that the explosions had excavated

a huge trench all around the bone –
which was even broader and longer
than he had been expecting. Most of it
was covered in mud, but it looked as
though the missiles had accidentally
blown a couple of holes in it.

At last the heli-gator stopped firing.
The smoke from the blasts hid Plog as
he crept closer. He saw a door open in
the side of the heli-gator – then a dozen
gators slid down the winch line to
attach the grappling hook to the huge
hunk of ivory.

"Oi! Gators!" Plog yelled. "Before you
pick up that bone – I've got a bone to
pick with you!" As the reptiles looked
over, he opened fire with a slime-shooter
– showering them with stinky water.

"Way to go, Fur-boy!" yelled Zill; she and Danjo galloped out from some muddy bags nearby. "But save some for us, OK?"

"No problem!" Plog tossed over his friends' shooters.

"Under attack!" wailed a soggy gator. His gruesome gang pulled out pistols and shot teeth in all directions. Zill and Danjo returned fire with the revolting liquid. Still half hidden by the smoke, Plog raced round in a large circle, firing short bursts, trying to make it seem as though the bone was surrounded by many mighty monsters. He saw Zill and Danjo sneaking up on the gators, ready for close-range combat — but then an unexpected missile came rocketing down in front of them. *BOOOOM!*

"No!" yelled Plog. His friends were

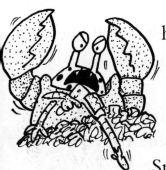

hurled backwards by the
blast – and lay still.
"Ssso – you ssstill
ssstruggle on, eh?"
boomed the Duke of
Snap over the heli-gator's
loudspeakers. "What does it take to
make you heroic fools give up?"

"More than you've got!" Plog
bellowed back. Then he gulped at the
sound of six more missiles flying through
the air. As they tore into the
ground close by, booming and
banging and filling the forest
with fire and smoke, Plog
squeezed under the huge
muddy bone for protection
until the bombardment stopped.
"Please let Zill and Danjo be
OK," he muttered fervently. "Please!"

"Enemies zapped," one gator
announced at last. "Bone-snatch can
continue. Grappling hook in position."

75

"Then let's get back to base with our prize," the Duke said happily. "At last the operation can begin!"

Operation? Plog wondered.

Then the giant bone started to rise into the air! Plog knew that if he was spotted, he'd be blasted instantly – so he dropped his slime-shooter, grabbed hold of one of the two holes drilled through the hard white bone, and clung on. Soon he was dangling above the ground. With a rush of relief, he saw Zill and Danjo stirring on the battleground. But by the time he was sure they were OK, the heli-gator and its prize had risen high, high into the air.

A fall from this height would kill me, Plog realized, fighting to keep his handholds as Snap and his army rocketed away. *Wherever the Duke's base might be — it looks like I'm going there too — with no friends, no slime . . . and no hope!*

Chapter Seven
INTO THE UNDERZONE

"Plog!" Danjo struggled up from the blasted ground and pulled Zill to her feet. "Plog, come back!" he called. But already, their dangling friend was barely visible. "I don't believe it – Snap's got him!"

"If only we'd managed to dodge those stupid missiles," groaned Zill, "we might have been able to save him."

Just then, Furp came bounding out of the Slime-mobile in a state of great excitement. "Danjo! Zill! Stop whatever you're doing and—" He bounced to a puzzled halt. "Whatever are you doing?"

"We're watching Plog get carried away to who knows where," said Zill miserably, pointing after the disappearing heli-gator. "He was holding onto that giant bone when Snap took it away."

Furp stared in horror. "Oh no! He'll get himself killed!"

"We have to go after him," cried Danjo.

"I'll drive us," said Zill. "PIE can track Plog for us, right? He's all-seeing . . ."

"But even he can't peep into the Murky Badlands, where the Duke of Snap has his base. Poor Plog will be completely lost." Furp started hopping up and down in alarm, and there was a clunk of glass objects from his metal pants.

"What can we do? Even if that cure I gave him works and his slime returns, he won't stand a chance . . ."

"Chill and be still," said Danjo, grabbing Furp in mid-air. "What do you mean, *cure*? And what's all that noise in your pants?"

"Pants?" Furp looked down and squeaked. "Great gonkberries! I almost forgot to say – I think I've found the cure for our lack of sliminess—"

"You have?" Zill thrust her snout into Furp's face. "Then, give! Give!"

"Yeah!" Danjo lunged for Furp's round metal pants. "Splash out the potion – get our slime in motion!"

"Wait!" Furp back-flipped out of his friends' reach – and the commotion in his pants grew louder. "Oh no! Now I've muddled up the order." He reached inside and extracted three identical bottles, each filled with a pale-green liquid. "Now, whose was whose?"

"Does it matter?" Zill asked impatiently.

"Of course it matters!" Furp cried. "It's like I said before – your slime is different from Danjo's slime, and mine is different again. So we each need a cure with a slightly different formula."

Zill groaned. "And you didn't think to stick labels on those bottles?"

"I wasn't expecting to get so shaken up," said Furp sheepishly.

"Well, with Plog in danger we can't afford to waste time," Danjo declared. "Our slimy powers are the only thing that might save him – so dish that splish!"

With a sigh, Furp studied the bottles
closely. "This one is probably Zill's . . .
And this one's a paler green, which
could mean it's mine . . . or Danjo's . . .
Or maybe *this* one is Zill's, and mine is
the one with the—"

"Make up your mind!" Zill yelled.

Furp thrust one bottle into her paw
and another into Danjo's pincer. "There.
I think that's right."

"Let's find out," Zill murmured.

The three friends glugged down the
gloop in a couple of gulps.

"Yuck!" spluttered Zill. "That tasted
like a bug's bottom."

Danjo licked his lips. "Mine tasted like
chip fat. Not bad!"

"And mine tasted like . . ." Furp
clutched his throat. "Grlghph!"

"What does 'grlghph' taste
like?" Danjo wondered.
"I've never had it—
Yeeoww!"

The crimson crab-monster suddenly gasped and clutched his belly. "My guts . . . they feel like they're on fire!"

"Everything's spinning . . ." Zill's tail drooped and her legs buckled beneath her. "What's happening?"

Furp hopped in the air – and landed on his head. *CLUNK!* "I don't know," he groaned. "I don't understand . . ."

"Seems clear to me." Danjo slumped to the ground. "You picked the wrong potions, Furp. They aren't curing us – they're *killing* us!"

Already far away from his stricken
friends, Plog was clinging onto the
muddy old bone for dear life. Slowly,
every muscle straining, he hauled
himself up inside one of the
two holes in the narrow
end of the thick white
slab and held on tight.
His bare feet, hanging
down in the freezing
air, soon grew numb,
and after an hour or
more he had lost all
feeling in his furry fingers too.

Thick swirling fog signalled the
borders of the Badlands. The heli-gator
ploughed into it. *We must be getting close
to Snap's lair*, thought Plog with a
shudder. *Even if I can get out of this scrape
– how will I ever find my way back home?*

Soon Plog glimpsed a sprawling wooden
palace, half submerged in swampland and

thick black mud. The heli-gator began to dip lower and lower, towards the mouth of a waterlogged sewer tunnel. Carefully it lowered the jumbo bone into the filthy water. Plog grimaced as the thick gloop covered his body up to the waist.

"Hear me, my gators," Snap's voice boomed from the speakers of his flying machine. "At last we hold the final part of my grand design . . . Place it in position while I park the heli-gator. I shall meet you in the Underzone – where the operation shall sssoon begin!"

Suddenly, to Plog's horror, dozens of alligator-men swarmed out of the wooden buildings and swam into the water.

Then they began guiding the bone away through the mucky stream.

Bewildered and bedraggled, Plog held on tight inside his narrow hidey-hole. *If they catch me*, he thought, *they'll eat me alive!*

The light faded and the sky became brickwork. Flickering lamps in the ceiling lit the way in flashes as the tunnel stretched deeper underground and the water grew thicker, greener and gloopier. The colossal bone was sinking into the sludgy liquid, and Plog with it – he had to use his snout as a snorkel, snuffling down the stale air.

Over the splashing of bone and bodies in the gunk, he could hear the sound of heavy grinding gears and the blips and blops of strange devices . . .

"Steady there!" hollered a gator. "Careful . . . push it along . . . a little bit more . . ." *WHUMP!* The bone finally came to rest amid many cheers.

Cautiously, Plog pushed his head out of the bone-hole and sneaked a look. "So *this* is the Underzone . . ."

The bone had been placed at a crossroads in the sewer course. The side-tunnels to Plog's left and right had been blocked off and turned into control rooms: platforms had been built over the nasty water, and these were covered in desks and screens and strange equipment, attended by gators in snazzy white lab coats.

Great hulks of rusting machinery lay at the edges of the main sewer ahead of him, beginning on either side of the big broad bone in which he was hiding, and stretching far into the distance. Plog suddenly saw that this tunnel was filled with many other bones, laid end to end in a careful, deliberate pattern.

Like a skeleton, he thought with a chill. And now that the mud had been washed away, he realized that the bone that held him could only be a strange, elongated skull. Two gaping sockets glared at him blankly. *Whatever this thing*

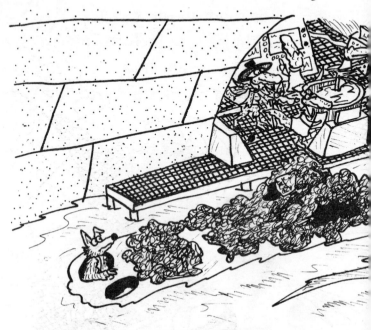

is, thought Plog, *I've been hiding in one of its nostrils!*

Then, suddenly, a familiar snarling howl echoed out. Plog turned to find that the Duke of Snap, resplendent as ever in mask, cloak and cane, had swept onto the left-hand platform through a hole in the brickwork. He was accompanied by Sabre, who was still chewing one of Plog's iron boots. Then the gator-wolf dropped it and started sniffing the air hungrily.

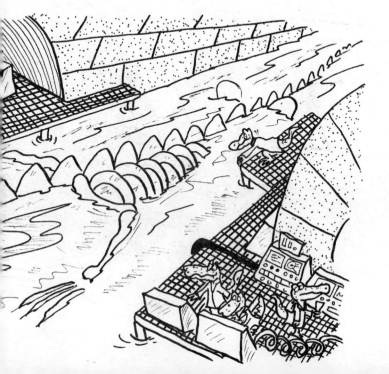

"What's the matter, my pet?" hissed
Snap. "Have you caught a ssscent?
Could it be . . . the sssmell of an
intruder?"

Yes, it could, Plog thought grimly. *And
if Sabre finds me, it's game over!*

With a slavering howl, the scaly beast
leaped off the platform, making straight
for Plog's hiding place . . .

Chapter Eight

BAD TO THE BONES

Sabre landed lightly on top of the skull, claws gripping and jaws slobbering. *My only hope's a surprise attack*, Plog decided. Taking a deep breath, he popped out of the nostril-hole – and punched Sabre on the snout!
The gator-wolf staggered back with a howl and landed in the gloopy water.

"It's Plog!" roared the Duke of Snap.

91

"Catch him, my minions! Crush him! Bring him to me – *now*!"

Plog jumped off the huge, horrible skull and started swimming back up the tunnel the way he'd come, hoping to reach the exit – but the water was so thick, he felt as if he were moving in slow-motion. Snap's white-coated gators dived in after him. Sleek and scaly, they cut a far swifter path through the gloopy liquid than Plog could hope to. At least twenty were zooming towards him.

In desperation, Plog waded over to the side of the sewer and started to climb the crumbling brickwork. But the gators fired more of their toothy bullets. Dust and stone erupted from the wall all around Plog – and an especially sharp fang jabbed him in the bottom.

"Yeoww!" he yelled, and lost his grip, plunging into the putrid water. *SPLOSH! WHACK!* He banged his head on a brick beneath the surface and swallowed a mucky mouthful that left him choking for breath. Dizzily, he saw the gators crowding around him. One of them had a large wooden club clutched in its mouth.
Plog tried to swim away once more, but – *WHOP!* – the club cracked down on his head. He saw a flash of stars – then blackness.

When Plog woke up, he soon wished he could go straight back to sleep.

He was lying on the left-hand platform, propped up in a big bucket of thick, soupy water. A pair of seagull's feet and a rotten fish tail stuck out of the cold salty mix, and the niff was nearly enough to knock his nose off. Plog coughed and groaned and shook his head to clear it – and realized that his wrists and ankles were manacled.

"Ssso . . ." hissed the Duke of Snap. "Our prisoner awakes!"

Plog shivered at the sound of the cold, familiar voice. Snap was glaring down at him, Sabre at his side, surrounded by hench-gators. Plog looked around for any possible escape route, but all he could see were gator-men, both on this platform and the one opposite, hosing down the enormous skeleton with giant jets of green goo.

"What's going on?" Plog demanded.
He tried to stand up but slipped, and a
seagull toe almost poked
his eye out. "Why have
you put me in this slop
bucket?" He gulped as a
horrible thought struck
him. "You're going to
eat me, aren't you?"

"Me? Eat YOU?" Snap
scoffed. "Really, Plog. I'm not an
animal."

"You are," Plog pointed out. "You're
an alligator."

"I am *far more* than that," hissed Snap,
eyes and teeth agleam. "Let me tell you
a little ssstory, Plog. Long ago, there
lived a pair of baby alligators who
escaped from a human zoo and
ssscuttled down here to the sssewers.
They grew big and fat and bred many
more great alligators . . . but toxic
radiation buried in this wasteland

mutated their eggs. A new breed began to hatch – clever, sssmarter, and ssso much more ssstylish. Alligators like *me* . . ."

"Yeah, rubbish alligators who never grew any bigger," said Plog. "You're a mutant titch!"

"Sssilence!" Snap roared, and the other gators cringed in fear. "I may be ssssmall but my brain is big. And while we may lack the power of our ancestors – the Great Alligators who escaped here ssso many years ago – that is sssoon to change."

"What do you mean?" Plog glanced again at the intricate ivory design dripping in sludge. "Why have you been gathering these old bones?"

"*Old bones?*" screeched Snap. "Those are the priceless pieces of my grand design.

97

The complete ssskeleton of the last Great Alligator." He leaned on his cane and lowered his voice. "Years back, a great flood ssswept his remains all over Trashland, buried them under waste and rubbish . . ."

"Best place for them, if you ask me," said Plog. "If you're that fond of your great alligator ancestor, and you've spent all this time piecing him back together, why are you covering him in all that gunk?"

"Because that 'gunk', as you call it, will help bring him back to life," said Snap reverently. "The machinery ranged on either ssside of his ssskeleton was designed by Lord Klukk. He planned to make a race of giant chickens to help him take over the land – but lacked the vital, life-giving ingredients for sssuccess."

"Ingredients that you had, I suppose?" sneered Plog.

"Of course!" Snap said fiercely. "I'm cleverer than that beaky old twerp ever was! I offered to share my discovery with Klukk in exchange for the use of his equipment, but he refused, and built a bionic chicken-bot instead."

"I know: the Slime Squad fought it and won," said Plog. "And once we'd got rid of him, you helped yourself to his secret stuff."

"Yes! And I have put it to marvellous use!" Snap chuckled. "Now the grand design of the ssskeleton is complete, the operation can begin. First, I shall bring the Great Alligator to life . . . and then I shall place my brilliant brain inside his body!"

"You're nuts!" cried Plog. "No one can perform a brain transplant!"

"No one except ME!" Snap guffawed. "Imagine the power I will possess! The tiny monsters of Trashland will fear me, ssserve me and fill my belly."

Plog was appalled. "You can't eat innocent monsters!"

"Not all of them, no," Snap agreed. "I will ssspare sssome to make me a giant hat, cape and eye-mask – and more will be needed to create a colossal cane . . ."

"You're bonkers," said Plog simply. "If you bring that thing to life, what's to stop him eating you and your army straight away?"

"Because he will eat that bucket of ssslop you're in first," said Snap, an evil glint in his eye. "It is drugged. It will sssend him to sssleep ssso that the operation can begin. And of course, he will eat you too . . ."

One of the gators wearing a lab coat came rushing up. "All bones gooed up, your dukeness," it hissed. "We are ready to switch on the life ray."

"Then do it!" Snap burst into peals of loopy laughter. "At last, the hour of the Great Gator has arrived!"

The Duke's cackling echoed around the sewers as the huge machines hummed into life. Plog stared, petrified, as an eerie green glow engulfed the skeleton and its dreadful bones began to twitch . . .

Chapter Nine
BONE IDOL!

The glow grew greener. The hum of power swelled to a buzzing thrum, like thousands of wasps trapped in a giant jam jar. Plog's fur stood on end as he saw scaly flesh begin to thicken around the sludge-spattered bones.

"It's working!" The Duke of Snap whooped with delight. "Working!"

But then the energy hum crackled and cut out. The green glow faded, and the half-formed flesh began to drip away like melting ice cream.

"Noooo!" Snap screamed. "What's happened to the power?"

"Perhaps you didn't pay your electricity bill?" came a froggy-sounding voice.

Plog gasped. Like Snap and Sabre and all the other gators, he turned in amazement – to find Furp bobbing about on the gloopy sewer water in an old matchbox.

"YOU!" screeched Snap.

"And me!" called Zill, breaking the surface of the thin sludge beside the opposite platform –

holding an electric plug on the end of a long black cable. "Guess what – I seem to have disconnected your power supply."

"But don't worry — *I've* got plenty of power for you and your gator gang," growled Danjo, jumping up onto the platform where Plog was imprisoned. 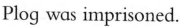 "The power of slime — to the max!"

"Fool!" jeered Snap, as Sabre growled in warning. "I took away your ssslimy abilities, remember?"

"But now we've got them back!" Furp proclaimed. "You see, I reversed your anti-slime with *anti*-anti-slime."

"And that's how we found your secret base," Zill added. "While Plog was dangling from your bone, his feet started dripping slime onto the ground below . . ."

"They did?" Plog grinned. "My tootsies were so cold, I couldn't feel them!"

"Well, we could sure smell them," said Danjo, shuddering. "So we simply jumped into the Slime-mobile and followed our noses! The trail led to this sewer, so we floated the rest of the way."

"Well, it's the last thing you will *ever* do," Snap hissed. "My gators have ssstudied your powers – and know how best to overcome them." He pointed his cane at a different group of gators. "You ten – muzzle Zill. You ten – catch the frog. And as for YOU . . ." He turned to Danjo. "My trusty SSSabre can stand up to your hot *and* cold ssslime – get him, my pet! *Attack!*"

Desperately, Plog strained to break free as the gator platoons dived into the sewer to menace Furp and Zill, and Sabre jumped at Danjo, jaws stretching wide . . .

But to everyone's amazement, Danjo spat out a slime-line and lassoed Sabre's mouth shut! The next moment he used it to swing the gator-wolf round and round like a scaly  wrecking ball, scattering the remaining gators like skittles, until finally he let go. Sabre went flying through the air and smashed into the soggy skeleton in an explosion of goo.

"But . . ." Snap stared in disbelief and horror. "But *you* don't ssspit ssslime-lines! Zill does!"

"Not right now she doesn't!" Zill cried. She waited until the speeding gators were almost on top of her – then jumped out of the water and clung to the wall, sticking with all six of her paws like the poodle-skunk version of Furp! The gators couldn't stop in time and smashed into the stonework before sinking out of sight.

"Impossible!" squeaked Snap. "Furp's the one who ssscales buildings with his ssslimy palms and feet . . ."

"Think so?" Furp and his bobbing matchbox were already surrounded by a ring of gators. "Check *this* out!" Suddenly blasts of blazing hot slime burst from his feet – propelling him high into the air! The reptiles raged and roared as splashes of sizzling slime scorched their scaly skin – and then Furp turned in mid-air to fire whooshes of freezing slime from his fingertips.

He turned the green gators into big blue ice-cubes – and dropped down to land neatly on top of one. "How's that?"

While Snap stared in horror, Danjo spat out a second slime-line that wound about the Duke's ankles – then he yanked on it hard and jerked the snappy dresser into the drink. *SPLOSH!*

Snap thrashed about in utter outrage. "My cape! My hat! They're ruined!"

"Along with your rotten plans," said Furp, splatting Snap in the face with an icy slime-ball that knocked him out – quite literally – cold.

"Here you go, Plog!" Danjo used his pincers to chop through Plog's manacles, then tipped him out of the yucky bucket onto the platform.

"I don't get it!" said Plog, grinning in baffled wonder. "What's happened to you all?"

"Just as I told Snap, we got our powers back." Furp strode through the filthy water to the platform on ice-slime stilts. "But I muddled up the cures – so we got *each other's* powers!"

"Luckily it helped take these gator-goons by surprise," said Zill, scampering over the ceiling like a peculiar spider. "Handy when you're outnumbered— *Ugh!*" She slapped two paws over her nose. "That whiff . . ."

"Plog!" Danjo groaned. "It's your feet!"

"Wow, it is too!" Plog looked down at his ugly furry tootsies. Now that they were out of the water they were oozing yellowy slime faster – and more stinkily – than he'd ever known. "Sorry – they've been safely in water since I got here." He scooped up his chewed metal boot and a small metal bucket, filled them with sewer water, then shoved his feet inside. "My slime's even stronger than it was before."

"Well, it's been blocked up for a while," Furp said. "You'll get back to normal."

"I only hope *we* do," said Zill, climbing down the wall to join them. "I want my old powers back."

"Me too," said Danjo. "Slime-lines taste like wee!"

"*Mine* don't," Zill informed him.

"Hang on," said Plog, suddenly anxious. "Where did the Duke of Snap go?"

"We left him in the water," said Furp, peering around – there were lots of gators floating about, but Snap wasn't one of them. "I wonder where he went . . . ?"

Suddenly the sprawling machines that ran the length of the sewer walls came juddering back to life. Emerald sparks flew across the sticky water as the molten mess that was the Great Alligator skeleton once again trembled with eerie life.

"Ha!" The Duke of Snap popped up from beneath the water just as Zill had done, his cloak clinging to his shoulders, his hat skew-whiff. "Two can play at that game – quite literally." All at once Sabre burst out of the water beside him. "That cable you unplugged – SSSabre and I have plugged it back in again!"

"There are other ways to put your machines out of action," cried Furp. Leaning back, balancing on his metal pants, he raised his legs and shot fiery-hot slime from the soles of his feet clear across the sewer. It showered the machines on one side of the wall. They fizzed and sparked . . .

But then the hum of energy grew deafeningly loud, and the green glow blazed greater still.

"Oh no," Furp cried, seeing the floppy flesh on the skeleton grow harder, fatter, scalier. "I haven't stopped the machines – I've caused a power surge!"

Plog watched helplessly as huge yellow teeth pushed out through crimson gums and beady black eyes swelled up in the skull's gaping sockets. The gooey bag of bones was becoming a solid scaly monster!

"Sssplendid!" roared Snap, while Sabre barked with laughter. "Thanks to you, the Great Gator is re-forming faster than I ever dreamed possible. Behold his becoming!"

The Great Gator slowly opened its dripping jaws. Plog looked helplessly at his team-mates . . .

But then the life-bringing machines finally overloaded, bursting apart in a huge turquoise explosion that threw Plog, Zill, Furp and Danjo clear across the platform. Smoke filled the air as a thundering *BOOM!* nearly tore Plog's ears off . . .

As the echoes of the blast faded, the Squaddies scrambled up – to hear a deep, croaking sigh echo from the smoky gloom.

"Uh-oh," said Danjo, as a brutish reptilian head appeared.

Plog stared, speechless with horror, at the gigantic monster before him. Its flesh glowed a sickly green. Its body was bloated, its scales misshapen. Its breathing came in great, grating rasps.

"Great Gator!" boomed the Duke of Snap. "I, who have brought you back to life, welcome you . . ."

The huge alligator ignored him completely.

"Er, Snap . . . ?" Furp called. "Real gators can't talk."

"This one will, once I've placed my brain inside his head!" Snap glared at Plog. "The operation must proceed at once."

"How are you going to put him to sleep?" Plog enquired. "Danjo's tipped over your bucket of drugged slops."

"But *you* were sssoaking in it for quite sssome time." Snap sniggered. "If the Great Gator eats you, he should ssstill be put to sssleep!"

"No way!" Zill shouted.

"While I have SSSabre there is *always* a way!" Snap turned to his pet. "Fetch me Plog – in as many pieces as you like. Fetch him NOW!"

Chapter Ten

CRUNCH TIME

With a fierce growl, Sabre streaked
towards the platform like a scaly
torpedo. But as if reacting to the sudden
movement, the Great Gator lunged
forward, opened his jaws around the
scaly gator-wolf – and then
slammed them shut.

"NO!" screamed
Snap, as the
Great Gator
started to
chew. "Ssspit
SSSabre out!
Quickly!
Please!"

But the monster just burped in Snap's face.

Zill gasped. "Did you see that?"

"I wish I hadn't," Plog admitted, feeling sick.

"Super-gross," Danjo agreed.

"Uh-oh," said Furp. "Look, those gators I put on ice – the blast must have thawed them out!"

While Snap gnashed his teeth and wailed with sorrow for his pet, his reviving army gazed up at the Great Gator in awe. "Hail the Great One!" they cried. "Hail the scaly king!"

"I don't think those little gators should get so close to their Great One," said Furp, closing his eyes. "As we've just seen, in the natural world, grown alligators are very happy to eat—"

CHOMP! GULP! SCROFF!

"– smaller alligators," Furp concluded.

Plog grimaced as the monster

advanced and slurped up the lab-coated
figures as if they were tasty morsels in
sewage soup. He tried to keep track of
Snap in all the chaos, but it was no
good: the Duke had disappeared. Some
of the little mutants splashed around in
a panic, trying to swim to safety, but the
Great Gator was too fast and too
deadly.

Suddenly, as if gripped by a terrible
thirst, the huge beast started washing
down his meal with the gloopy water
around him. *GULP! GOLP!*

"I don't believe it," Danjo cried. "He's
draining the sewer dry!"

"Do normal alligators drink as much as that?" asked Zill. "He's getting bigger all the time!"

Plog saw that she was right – the Great Gator was inflating. His bogey-coloured skin was stretched tight, ready to burst. He looked more like a giant scaly balloon than a real alligator.

"The power surge in the machines must have boosted his growth," said Furp. "His new body still craves energy – so he's eating and drinking anything in sight."

"I think you're right." Plog gulped as the Great Gator turned his horrible head towards them. "And what's more . . . I think we might be next on the menu!" The overstuffed beast began lumbering in their direction. "Time to shift – NOW!"

Making the most of their new-found powers, the Squad attempted their escape. Zill scampered away along the side of the sewer wall like a poodle-skunky bug. Furp squirted jets of hot slime from his heels to propel himself clear. Danjo spat out a slime-line at the ceiling and swung away. All three pitched up in the middle of the muddy sewer-bed.

But Plog tripped as the metal bucket slipped off his foot. He landed flat on his snout! At once, his exposed foot began pumping out thick smelly slime. The Great Gator blundered closer, his huge jaws snapping . . .

"Enjoy your trip, Plog?" Like a super-athlete, Danjo swung down on another slime-line and scooped up his grateful friend. "I'll take you on another!"

And a split-second
after Danjo had
whizzed Plog out of
reach—
SMASSSSH!
The Giant Gator
bit right through the
platform and gulped
it down, controls,

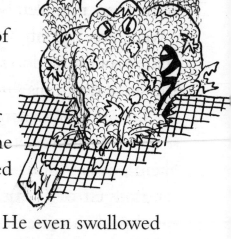

equipment and all. He even swallowed
Plog's thick puddle of slime. But then his
scaly skin broke out in black blotches,
and another massive belch escaped from
his gaping mouth.

Danjo landed with Plog beside Furp
and Zill. "What do we do?" Zill panted.
"We'll never outrun that thing."

"Perhaps we can slow him down,"
said Furp. "That gruesome gator's
stuffed himself sick – and Plog's
disgusting super-slime seems to be
giving him indigestion. If we could only
feed him some more of it . . ."

Plog kicked off his remaining, mangled boot. "Well, there's plenty to spare – but how do we get the slime down his throat?"

"Like this!" Danjo spat out another slime-line and swung with Plog right over the Great Gator's head. As he opened his jaws, Plog shook his feet and showered him with slime. The beast spat and hissed, his tongue inflating like a balloon.

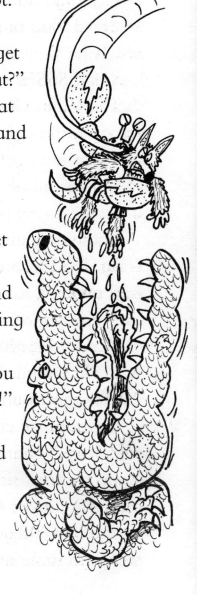

"Plog, I can't hold you if you wriggle like that!" Danjo yelled.

"Let him drop," called Furp. "I'll give him a slimy crash mat!" As good as his word, he sprayed out a chunky

mound of slush beneath Plog – who
landed *SPLAT!* in its middle and skidded
wildly across the sewer-bed on the slimy
ice. As he went, he started kicking out his
legs as if dancing the can-can, and his
shoe-goo flew down the Great Gator's
throat in thick yellow blobs.

"Grab my tail, Fur-boy!" cried Zill,
racing alongside him. "I'll give you
a tow!"

Plog did as she asked. As the Great
Gator tried to bite him in half again,
Zill hauled him away with her black
and white brush – and dragged him
right up the wall! Holding on for dear
life, Plog waggled his feet again. A slimy
shower rained down on the gator, but
in his keenness to devour Plog his
jaws stayed open. As the yellow
gloop trickled down his throat, his
legs grew larger, his belly bigger,
his thrashing tail more and
more titanic. The whole sewer

124

shook and shuddered as the Great
Gator's bloated, bulging body began to
smoulder and smoke, until finally –
KER-BLAMMMM!
The alligator blew himself apart, and
his freaky flesh turned instantly to ashes.
The dark flakes scattered like confetti
over the length of the dried-out,
crumbling tunnel.

For a while, all Plog, Danjo, Furp and Zill could do was stare in wonder and disbelief.

Then they cheered!

Zill lowered Plog to the ground, Danjo swung down and passed Plog his mangled footwear. Furp hopped across to join them on another hot blast of slime.

"We did it!" Danjo beamed.

"Thanks to Furp," said Plog proudly. "Without his cures we'd still be slimeless."

"I muddled things up, though, didn't I?" said Furp, looking down ruefully at his icy hands.

"If you hadn't," said Zill, "we'd never have taken Snap by surprise."

"Hey, what happened to Snap, anyway?" said Plog, peering around. "Where'd he go?"

"Nowhere pretty." Danjo pulled a face and pointed further along the dried-out, ashy tunnel. Plog saw that while the Great Gator's life had been brief, the beast had still had time to do a poo. The brown mess was lying on the ground. And sticking out from inside it were a few scraps of cloak and a diamond-topped cane . . .

"Ugh!" Plog looked away. "What a horrid way to go."

"Snap was hungry for power," said Furp quietly, "but his newborn beast was just hungry!"

"After that little workout, I'm feeling kind of hungry myself," said Danjo. "Come on, the Slime-mobile's waiting outside . . . last one back has to clean out the lav-lab!" He coughed and spat and jerked his head to zing out a slime-line – but nothing came out. "Hey, what gives? Don't tell me my slime's gone again?"

Zill tried jumping onto the wall – and immediately fell down in a heap. "Oh no! Furp, you never said your cure wouldn't last!"

"I don't understand. Let me test mine . . ." Furp jumped up high on jets of fiery slime – until they spluttered and stopped.

128

"Whoaaaa!" He flailed about in mid-air, but then touched the sewer wall with his fingers – and stuck tight! "Hey, my *real* slimy powers ..." He quickly scuttled down the wall. "They've come back!"

"I wish *mine* would." Zill cleared her throat – and a tiny thread of slime flicked out of her poodly jaws. "Hey, d'you see that? I wonder ..." She shook her head, gave an enormous, hacking cough – and a thick, strong slime-line whooshed out to splat against the wall. "Yayy!" She grabbed Plog in a hug. "My spit's back in business!"

"Fascinating!" Furp beamed with delight. "It would seem that our natural slime varieties have reasserted themselves."

"Mine haven't yet," Danjo grumbled, staring into his pincers. "Come on . . ." He heaved and strained as if pushing out a plop. "Come *on*!" Suddenly both pincers unblocked in a steaming rush of hot-and-cold slime, squirting Danjo in the face so hard that he fell over. "Oh, YES!" he spluttered, wiping his eyes. "I've got the old magic back too!"

"I'm so glad we've regained our powers." Plog smiled. "But in a way,

I'm pleased we lost them for a while.
It proved that however bad things get,
we'll always have each other."

"You betcha," said Danjo.

"We're a team," Furp agreed.

"Now and always." Zill high-fived her
three friends. "Whatever we face,
whatever the odds . . . it's the Slime
Squad for ever."

Plog smiled. "And will we be beaten?
NEVER!"

The Slime Squad will return in
THE SLIME SQUAD vs THE CONQUERING CONKS